Paul Smith & Ken Taylor

GERMAN SECRETS
Achtung to Zeitgeist

Illustrated by Bernhard Foerth

ISBN: 978-3-8391-9229-0

Edited by PSA International, Salgen, www.psa-international.de
Illustrations: Bernhard Förth, Munich, www.bernhard-foerth.de
Typesetting: Stefan Schiessl, Dachau, www.schiessldesign.de
Print & Distribution: Books on Demand, Norderstedt, www.bod.de

Printed in Germany

Dedication

To all our German friends as a "Danke schön"
for being so tolerant and understanding of us –
and for providing most of the contents!

List of Contents

Part 1 – Impressions

Part 2 — Survey Results

Appendix

Introduction

Living and working in Germany has been pleasurable and rewarding. We've met a great many interesting and friendly people. We've learnt a lot from them. And this is our "British" way of repaying this friendship and hospitality.

"German Secrets" is not intended as an academic dissection of Germany and the Germans, there are enough of those. On the contrary, this book is meant to be an affectionate and fun kaleidoscope of some of our impressions, and also an opportunity for Germans to talk about Germans.

The book is divided into two sections:

Part 1: Various impressions, presented alphabetically and in no order of importance. Dip in anywhere!

Part 2: A summary of "The Real Truth about The Germans", an online survey carried out on One-Word-A-Day (www.owad.de), a free English vocabulary learning service. The survey addresses the question: "Do the Germans see themselves as others see them?" and provides some interesting answers.

An old and rather tired joke starts with the question "Where would we be without a sense of humour?" the answer is "Somewhere in Germany!" We have a problem with this stereotype - we've had more fun in Germany than in many other countries. This book is the result of our 30 year joint venture with thousands of Germans - friends, colleagues, and business partners.

If you are a "foreigner," and have received this book from a German, this means two things:

1. They consider you a friend.

2. They most certainly <u>do</u> have a sense of humour.

Paul Smith & Ken Taylor

Salgen & London, October 2009

P.S.: If you have comments on the contents of this book, or suggestions for a future edition, drop us a line at: psa@smith.de in English, oder auf deutsch.

The survey "The Real Truth About the Germans" is still running online at: http://tinyurl.com/mu9mfd (but only in German). The results are continually aggregated and will be included in later editions of this book.

Part 1 – Impressions

Achtung!

Thanks to Hollywood films, comic strips, and the Rock Band U2, the German word "Achtung!" is now firmly embedded in the English language. And what a useful, life-saving word it can be. So much more concise and precise than its English cousins "Watch out!", "Be careful!" or "Pay heed, kind Sir!" If a light-flashing Porsche is bearing down on you at 240 kph, you don't want to mess around with unnecessary syllables.

Of course, we do use the word "attention" but never in the context of giving a warning or caution.

The following wordplay joke, originally broadcast on BBC Radio 4, has even been known to raise a smile in Germany. Tell it carefully:

A German farmer walks across a field, slips over in the mud, and falls face down into a cow pat. Rising to his feet, the only thing he can say is "Ach! Dung!"

Angst

The German soul is a very deep and troubled one. You only have to look at the works of Kant, Nietzsche, Hegel, Heidegger, Leibnitz, Marcuse or Schopenhauer to understand that it is not easy to understand.

It's best summed up by a very German word to describe a very German feeling: Angst.

Angst is more than just anxiety. It's searching the soul to determine the whole purpose of life. Who am I? Why am I here? What's it all for? (As Anglo-Saxon pragmatists we're inclined to add a fourth question: Who cares?)

Angst has even spilled into the German pop culture. It's the title of a well-known pop song by Herbert Groenemeyer that captures this deep-seated fear. It ends with the words: "So scared of being scared, we go to sleep."

Good night.

Beate Uhse

Walking along a typical German high street, between the clothes boutique and the Apotheke, you might come across a Beate Uhse sex shop. These shops are as much a shopping institution in Germany as Walmart in the United States and Marks and Spencers in the UK.

Beate Uhse was an amazing woman. She was a stunt pilot in the 1930s, flew transport aircraft in the Second World War (rising to the rank of captain) and then turned businesswoman as a young widow in the 1940s. Her mail order company gave women sexual advice and sold condoms. This simple beginning formed the basis for what is now the world's leading sex aid business.

When you go into a Beate Uhse shop (which we have done purely for research purposes of course) you will find four main sections. There

11

are individual booths showing pay-per-view porno movies (kept immaculately clean and with a plentiful supply of tissues). There is a huge selection of DVDs catering to all tastes and practices (some of which we didn't know existed). You can buy clothes for dressing-up games (the saucy maid is still a favourite). Finally, you will find a large assortment of sex aids and sex toys (what do they do with that!).

The customers are mainly, but not only, men. There is a particular "Beate Uhse" look when they come out of the doorway – eyes downcast and edging out of the shop sideways – just in case their neighbour happens to see them and notice the shape of the package they are carrying. In fact the shops provide anonymous-looking carrier bags to prevent anyone knowing where you have been shopping. But since they are easily recognised, the bags act more as an advertisement for the company than as a cover-up for the customer!

There is something frank and straightforward about the Beate Uhse approach that strikes a note with many Germans. When the wall came down in 1989, sales rocketed as a new pornography-starved market opened up. In 1999 Beate Uhse AG was the first erotic company to be listed on the German Stock Exchange. The share prices rose immediately (perhaps because the share certificates had two near-naked women on them).

Beate Uhse died in 2001, but her legacy can be studied at leisure in her pride and joy: The Beate Uhse Erotic Museum in Berlin.

(P.S.: We recommend the fluffy covered erotic handcuffs – excellent value and very good quality.)

Beer

There are about 1300 breweries in Germany (population 82 million), almost as many as there are in the United States (population 307 million). This shows you just how important beer is in the German culture.

Because of the ancient "purity order" from 1516, the beers are made with simple, clean, pure ingredients that allegedly guarantee no hangovers. However, having tested this with several litres of dark beer from the famous Bavarian monastery brewery at Andechs, we can categorically state that this is not the case.

There are many excellent German beers.
But there are four kinds we recommend you try:

1. **Hefeweizen.** This unfiltered wheat beer should be cold drunk on a summer evening in the English Garden in the centre of Munich. Be warned however. Two or three of these and your stomach feels like a Zeppelin – ready to float away over the city – or explode!

   In Bavaria it is traditionally drunk whilst eating white sausages and sweet mustard. This has to be before 12.00 noon. Traditionally the sausages can't be kept for more than a couple of hours, so you have to have them for breakfast. But why you have to have them with Hefeweizen beer at that time of the day only a Bavarian can tell you.

2. **Pils.** This is a slightly bitter, light, clean-tasting, clear beer popular in Northern Germany. There are two warnings here. First, the head is the same size as the body. This means you don't get much beer for your money. Second, a really good pils takes seven minutes to pour. So order the second and third pils when you order the first.

3. **Doppelbock.** This a very strong, very smooth, full-bodied dark lager. It's a great winter drink. But be careful. Most doppelbocks have more alcohol content than wine. Drink a few half-litres of sherry and you get the idea.

4. **Berliner Weisse.** This is a weak, sour wheat beer served with either a dollop of raspberry syrup or green woodruff syrup in something resembling an oversized cocktail glass. The similarity to a delicious cocktail ends there. It is not a pleasant drink but is worth trying anyway. After satisfying your curiosity, go back to sampling the other beers.

Bavaria considers itself the home of German beer. Indeed half the breweries in Germany are Bavarian. Beer is not viewed as an alcoholic drink in Bavaria, but is thought of as a loaf of bread. So go to one of the beer halls in Munich and have a Paulaner sandwiched between a Spaten and a Loewenbräu.

Bosses

The German boss is definitely the boss. He (it's usually a man) sits in his office with the door closed and sometimes even has lamps that light up outside to tell you he is busy. He usually is. He works hard. And he expects you to do the same and to show it with plenty of paperwork.

In meetings he speaks the most. Very few brave souls disagree when he has said what he thinks. You never interrupt him.

He expects you to have opinions on your specialist subject and to be quiet when the discussion moves on to other topics. He decides.

You rarely mix with your boss socially. An office Christmas meal or party is a rather formal affair (unlike British office parties where anything goes as long as you don't talk about it the next day). And even here he is always addressed by his title and name because by attending he is simply doing his duty.

If he doesn't sound like much fun – he's not supposed to. Business is serious business and it's his job to keep it that way.

Breakfast Rolls

A friend of ours gets up at six thirty every morning and cycles round to his local bakers to get his Breakfast Rolls. There's barely room to park the cycle outside. The bakery is crowded with shoppers. It's the breakfast roll rush hour (a breakfast roll jam?)

Dieter is a bread roll connoisseur. He knows exactly what he wants, how it should taste and where to buy it. If Frenchmen know their wine, Italians their pasta, Belgians their chocolate, then Dieter and millions of his fellow countrymen know their rolls.

They range from plain rye rolls to rolls covered in poppy seeds, sesame seeds, pumpkin seeds or caraway seeds to rolls covered in melted cheese, rolls sprinkled with sugar or nuts or grains or baked with sweet raisins. All of them are delicious and designed to make the German breakfast a meal for hearty eaters.

If you are weight or figure conscious, avoid your German baker in the mornings and have 30 minutes extra beauty sleep. Stick to your unsweetened muesli. Once you enter the bakery, the smell, look and finally the taste of the rolls will destroy any will power you may have. Your diet goes out of the door as you enter in.

Bureaucracy

Germans hate bureaucracy. Why? Because it's everywhere in German society. And they are the ones who suffer the most from it.

If you ever have to go through an official process like getting permission to extend or remodel your house – forget it! It involves unravelling Byzantine regulations and dealing with Kafkaesque officialdom.

If everyone complains about it and hates it so much, why don't they do something about it? It's because there is another, even more powerful side to the coin: the desire for order. Everything should be organised properly and everything needs to be written down so that all eventualities are covered. So, hating red tape is less important than making sure everything is done correctly. And is as it should be. Only then you can say those important words: "Alles in Ordnung".

Cars

An Englishman's home is his castle. For a German his castle is his car. It is every German man's inalienable right and duty to own the most expensive car he can afford on his salary. Even if he can't afford the next model up, he'll sell his wife and children to get it.

Cars are the ultimate status symbol. You simply need the right car to match your social standing. The car really should be German made. None of your Japanese and Korean economy models thank you.

The most popular make is VW, representing reliability, economy, and safety... but for status, speed, and pure driving comfort go for Audi, Mercedes, or BMW. For speed, go for Porsche.

Such a valuable status symbol should be looked after like an only child. Its health must be regularly checked and it has to be kept clean and well-groomed so that the neighbours will not gossip about neglect. Every Saturday morning, it has to be washed, polished and dusted inside and out until every last speck of dirt has been removed and the neighbour can see his reflection in the bodywork when he carries out his inspection.

It is also every German's inalienable right to drive as fast as possible at every opportunity, especially if they own a Porsche. Porsche owners feel they have the right to tailgate one metre behind a car doing only 200 kph in the outer lane of the autobahn. They should also have their indicator flashing to show the slowcoach in front that they need to make way for someone who is doing 240.

Foreign visitors must be aware that hand gestures indicating the stupidity of other drivers are a criminal offence in Germany. However badly you have been cut up by a BMW or tailgated by an Audi, keep your hands firmly on the wheel. You cannot be arrested for what you tell yourself or for what you imagine happening in a fairer world.

Cheers!

Imagine you are in a British pub with a group of friends. Your beer arrives. You pick it up and say, "Cheers!" One friend lifts his glass and says, "Cheers!" but does not drink. One nods and drinks with you. Two others continue chatting and break off briefly to mumble "Cheers!" and then continue their chat. None of them look you directly in the eye. All very casual.

You won't get away with this approach in Germany.

First of all, you have to make a big decision about which form of "Cheers!" to use. There is a whole hierarchy of words you can use.

"Prost!" is used with beer.

"Zum Wohl" is used with wine.

"Auf uns!" or "Auf Dich!" is used with cocktails.

"Und weg!" or "Hau'weg das Zeug!" is used with schnapps.

(There are also several vulgar variations. Drop us an email if you want to know what they are). It seems that all formalities disappear when the schnapps arrives. But if the drinkers are good friends you can still use "Prost!"

"Cheers!" is often used when drinking whisky or you can also say "Auf Schottland!" But as it's usually pretty late in the evening when the whisky appears, then anything goes.

There is also an important ritual you must follow to be an accepted member of the circle when saying "Cheers!" After choosing the correct toast, raise your glass to about head height and say it loudly. Your drinking companions will stop whatever they are doing, raise their glasses and repeat your toast. Look everyone directly in the eye before drinking whilst still holding your glass high. Then clink glasses. If you're drinking beer, clink the bottom part of the glass. For wine use the upper part. Purists even say there are different clinks for different beers. Only now can you drink. Then nod. Look at each other again. Relax.

Finally, take two or three furtive slurps of whatever you are drinking to recover.

Translations:

Prost!	Cheers!
Hau weg das Zeug!	Down the hatch!
Zum Wohl!	Your health!
Auf uns!	To us!
Auf Dich!	To you!
Und weg!	Bottoms up!

Christmas Markets

German towns have Christmas markets in December. They are marvellous affairs, especially if you like eating and drinking (which most Germans do). People brave the icy December weather to walk around a market square filled with small stands manned by people wearing six layers of clothes or looking as if they are about to take part in a ski competition.

You can buy all sorts of handicrafts (things you would never normally buy), trinkets (presents that people don't want or need), a huge variety of food (as long as you like pork), and plenty to drink (beer, schnapps and mulled wine). Ah! The mulled wine (Glühwein)! Delicious! It smells of winter, snowy days and Christmas. You queue up at the stall, pay your deposit on a mug and fill up with piping hot, spiced mulled wine. It warms you down to your toes. You stand at round cocktail-style tables and chat to your friends or to anyone else who happens to need a place to rest their mug. It's very easy drinking. Sometimes too easy. Glühwein is deceptively strong. When you drink it steaming hot on a cold night, it will sneak up on you. The urge to find a place to lie down and sleep will be great. And you might find you are fighting for a resting space with others who feel exactly the same way.

The most famous Christmas market is in Nuremberg, but many other towns and cities would dispute that claim. The markets are not just popular with the local population. You will also find busloads of British pensioners buying unusual presents for their grandchildren, Dutch families looking for Christmas bargains and Scandinavians propping up the bars and Glühwein stalls. There's something for everyone. It's a great way to build up your Christmas spirit in anticipation of the day itself.

Clubs

If you really want to be accepted into German society, join a club (Verein). Everyone is a member of something. These clubs range from normal sports clubs (one third of all Germans are members of such clubs) to choirs (10,000 of them) to hunting and shooting clubs (dating from the Middle Ages and full of tradition and ritual). Most clubs require only fees to join. With others an invitation from a member is needed.

Besides meeting people and making friends, club membership has other advantages:

- ↣ It allows you to meet like-minded people (and avoid the others).

- ↣ It allows you to feel part of an historic tradition (the oldest shooting club was founded in 1139). It gives you the chance do some social climbing (club chairmen have high status).

- ↣ It allows you to do things in a group, which you would never dare do alone in public (Belly dancing? Yodelling? Dressing up in archaic costumes?).

Most importantly, it gives you a sense of belonging. For some it provides a sense of exclusivity. There is an expression in German, "hier sind wir unter uns" – here we are among ourselves. Within the four walls of the club you no longer have to be on your best behaviour. You can relax and be yourself without fear of disapproval from the outside world.

Der - Die - Das

Can anyone explain why the German language needs three genders; masculine, feminine and neuter? Where English only uses the simple "the", German has three alternatives, Der Hund (the dog), die Katze (the cat), das Schwein (the pig). Der, Die, and Das make life so complicated for us foreigners. It's hard enough to remember the vocabulary without having to remember the gender and making the necessary agreements between words.

German is certainly not the only language with such complicated rules. But for a culture that prides itself on a straightforward and logical approach to life, it seems ridiculous.

For instance, the German for young boy is der Junge, that's OK. But young girl is das Mädchen. Why is it neuter?

Girls! You're feminine! Why don't you complain?

Details

Lack of attention to detail is not a fault commonly found in Germany. Simply attend a business presentation and you will soon understand what we mean. You will be bombarded for an hour with detailed facts, explanations of the facts and yet more explanations about the explanations, all accompanied by countless power point presentations packed with even more information.

This is often spoken or read in a low-key manner with little stress or emphasis (no show of emotions here please!). It's enough to send even the most dedicated businessman or woman to sleep. And it frequently does. This demand for detail runs through every part of life.

The queues at the train information desks are enormous. Why? Because each prospective passenger needs to know every possible route, every possible time and every possible price category for their trip in three months time. Meanwhile you are there trying to get information about tickets for a train leaving in five minutes time.

E-mails from German business colleagues are easy to recognise when you open them up. They are long. They have numbers and bullet points. There is not much white space on the screen. Manuals for German products and equipment describe in great detail uses and misuses that no one as ever thought of.

In the Apotheke you cannot simply buy a bottle of cough medicine. The assistant will shower you with questions about type of cough, known allergies, chronic illnesses, any other medication you take, your sexual preferences…(just kidding, we haven't heard that one yet). But you know exactly what you want because you bought a bottle there last week. If you don't speak German, they can do all this in flawless English.

They say "the devil is in the details." In other words you need to carefully examine things for hidden problems. In Germany this is done with enthusiasm and great thoroughness. It's a great strength, but it can also be mind-numbingly boring. In truth, the devil is the detail.

Dinner for One

Once a year in Germany the entire family settles down to watch a black and white television sketch in English called Dinner for One. It was written in the 1920s, recorded for German TV in 1963 and is now shown on several channels every New Year's Eve, which the German's call Sylvester. Unless you have spent Sylvester here, you have probably never heard of it. But according to the Guinness Book of Records it is the most repeated sketch on television.

It stars two well-known British actors (long since dead). The first viewing is hilarious. But it is hard to understand why Germans watch it year after year. They know the sketch by heart. They know every punch line. They know the names and personae of the various characters acted out by the ageing butler for his elderly mistress. The most famous punch line - The same procedure as every year - is regularly quoted whenever you are expected to repeat an activity.

What is it about this sketch that captures the German imagination in this way? Is it the humour of the situation? It's funny, but no funnier than countless other sketches. Is it the brilliance of the acting? The actors are very good, but so are plenty of others. Is it the playful, sexual undertone? You can find that everywhere now.

We believe it's the need for a non-threatening tradition; something warm and cuddly and funny that we can all refer to without any guilt. Repeated broadcasts have turned into it an annual tradition that is impossible to end.

Our thanks to Miss Sophie (May Warden) and James (Freddie Frinton) for giving Germany its yearly dose of collective laughter, and donating "Same procedure?" to the German language.

Directness

Here are two ways of saying the same thing. Which one is the German approach and which one is the British?

1. "Well I was wondering whether it might be at all possible for us to meet on the 29th or whether this might be a little inconvenient for you and it might be that you prefer some other date which is more suitable for you either earlier or later that week or do you have perhaps some other alternative?"

2. "I want to meet on the 29th."

Not too difficult a question to answer we think! Our German friends tell us to say what we mean and mean what we say. As British speakers of English we prefer to say what we think you want to hear and package it nicely!

Dogs

If you are allergic to dogs, don't go to Germany. They are everywhere. And so are the signs that they have been there. At your local restaurant you can find one or two dogs under tables with water bowls provided by the hosts. Your local beer garden is full of families with their several dogs. Get on the underground and be careful not to tread on some poor animal's paws.

It seems that dogs are the only creatures allowed to disturb the German need for order. Dogs give them a sense of anarchic freedom (as long as it is not taken too far and as long as you have your plastic poo bag with you).

The best way to befriend people in Germany is to take your dog for a walk. This offers the chance to meet other dog lovers (99% of the population), little old ladies who want to feed it, and children who want to pet and ride it.

In Germany dogs seem to come in two sizes. Either they are huge German Shepherd dogs or they are small, yappy lap dogs. You don't see many in between. The German Shepherds (and occasional Doberman) provide people with the macho feeling that they are preparing for the hunt and getting back to nature even if the dog has never seen a rabbit in its life. The lap dogs (poodles with bows in their hair or wriggling dachshunds) provide the soft love that might otherwise be missing.

So when visiting Germany, put on your dog-lover face, praise to the skies the doggies you meet and watch where you put your feet. Cave Canem.

Doktor

Germans are not as obsessed with titles as their Austrian neighbours. But they are still pretty obsessed.

You have to work long and hard to get your "Doktor" title, so it's important to show this hard work (and your intelligence and status) by using it on your business card, on seminar table place cards, in introductions and in the phone book.

In the south of Germany and Austria the wife of a doctor assumes his title by marriage and is entitled to be called "Frau Doktor" making her indistiguishable from her real female doctors.

In Britain and many other countries, the "Doctor" title is only used for medical doctors or in academic life. So it's rather surprising for the German "Doctor" (of Law or Business Administration) when he or she is asked to look at someone's swollen ankle during a business meeting in London.

Du and Sie

There is the well-known German joke where Helmut Kohl meets Margaret Thatcher and says, "Margaret, we know each other well now. Please, you can say "you" to me."

This makes no sense at all unless you know that there are two ways to say "you" in German – the formal Sie and the informal Du.

So how do we foreigners know when to use one form or the other?

1. Only God, children, pets, close friends, and family members are addressed as Du – other minor gods and the rest of the world are Sie. (Emails are sometimes written in the Du form for some reason, although this is by no means a universal rule. Maybe they are seen as some kind of American invention so that Anglo-Saxon rules apply.)

2. Use the formal Sie for adults you've just met or don't know very well - unless you end up in bed together. Then the formal Sie sounds a little awkward.

3. In business situations and with work colleagues. You might have known your colleagues for years and still call each other Sie, Herr and Frau. The exception is the same as for rule two.

4. When in doubt, use Sie. (That also includes the next day at work for the exception to rule 2.)

5. If someone offers to go over to using the Du form they are probably older than you or your social or work superior or both. You can't refuse. And you have to seal it with a drink. First you clink glasses and afterwards kiss each other on the cheek. Watch out for a more intimate variation, the so-called "Bruderschaft trinken" (Brotherhood drink) - this involves interlocking your glass-holding arms, drinking, and kissing on the mouth.

6. What do you say to your prospective mother-in-law when you first meet her? This is tricky. You don't want to sound too stiff and over-formal. After all she will soon be family. But you don't want to sound too familiar either. Best keep quiet and let her do the talking. (This is probably good general advice anyway.)

There are a couple of other tricky situations:

If you use Sie when the other person thinks you should use Du it can give the impression you are arrogant or angry.

Conversely, if you use Du when the other person thinks you should use Sie it comes across as insulting or superior.

Complicated isn't it? Our tip is to keep it in English until you have learnt all the rules!

Facial Hair

Most German men are clean-shaven. But there are exceptions. Some young men sport oddly shaped modern goatees, but that is simply a fashion.

Some men have full beards, but that might be because they are ex-hippies still living in 1959, or for religious reasons, or because they are down and outs hoping for a handout in the subway.

Some have droopy, Mexican bandit moustaches, but that is because they grew them in the 1970s and haven't bothered to shave them off, or because they are gay.

You could say the above about almost any European country. But there is one group of men who only appear in Germany. These are usually middle-aged and otherwise normal in appearance. But they sport Kaiser Wilhelm or King Ludwig facial hair – beautifully waxed pointed moustaches above superbly clipped pointed beards. The longer the moustache, the prouder the owner. And they love to twirl the moustache's pointed ends like a caricature villain in a melodrama. This is not a fashion. It's a statement. The problem is the statement is in German and the rest of us just don't get it.

Family

When German businessmen introduce themselves in international meetings they often start by saying something like this, "My name is Rainer Holtz. I am forty-two years old. I am married with two children." What he really means is that if he is forty-two then he obviously must have a wife and family.

The family is central to most German male's concept of a happy life: a cosy home, a loving wife, not too many kids but several pets. And they all live happily ever after in a beautifully furnished house. This is the concept of "Heimat," the traditional home and hearth. The wife should preferably be five years younger than him, be an excellent cook and stay at home when the kids are young and raise them as good Christians.

But the German Hausfrau has started to assert her independence and no longer fully accepts the traditional "Kuche, Kinder, Kirche" (The kitchen, the children, the church) role she once had.

Over 40% of Germany's workforce is female (although they are paid a lot less than the men). Women are forcing traditionally minded politicians to provide more child-care facilities so that they can keep working after their maternity leave (if you want that beautifully furnished home you need the double income).

More and more couples don't marry but simply live together (nearly 30% of babies are born out of wedlock). The divorce rate in Germany is no different to that of other major European countries (we all can make mistakes). And the birth rate is one of the lowest in Europe (maybe we shouldn't go into why that is).

So in future, Rainer will probably start his self-introduction by saying, "I am Rainer Holtz. I am forty-two years old. I live with a partner. We have no children but three dogs."

Food

Germans begin each meal with the words, "Guten Appetit". Translated directly it means "Good appetite". When you eat in Germany, that's exactly what you will need.

Germans like their food. Restaurants, cafes and ice cream parlours seem to do good business from breakfast to bedtime. And if you need a snack in between (which many do) there are also small kiosks where you stand to eat your bratwurst, pizza slice, pretzel (or all three) and have a beer (or two). There is a huge variety of traditional German fare on offer, if you like pork. You can have roast pork, braised pork, fried pork, pork schnitzel, pork stews, pork liver cheese (which has nothing to do with liver or cheese), pork ribs, pork tongue, pork belly, pork knuckles and stuffed stomach of pork! This was Helmut Kohl's favourite dish and he used it to test the courage of visiting VIPs.

Go to the food hall in the magnificent KaDeWe department store in Berlin for an array of pork sausages as far as the eye can see. You can buy a different sausage for every meal for a whole year. And by the look of the shopping baskets, that's what most of the customers plan to do.

"Spätzle" is a typical German pasta that can be served as a main meal on its own with melted cheese, or used to accompany your pork (or any other meat or fish). It means "little sparrows". That is not how we would describe the appetite of most people who eat it.

German dumplings can be savoury or sweet. Both versions lie heavily on the stomach and you will need a schnapps or a short lie-down after eating, or both. As you can see, traditional German food is not for the calorie conscious. But the bread is wonderful.

Football

As the old saying goes, "Football is a game between two teams of eleven players. And Germany win."

In Germany football is part sport, part life-style and part religion – correction – mainly religion.

Football is the one area of life that allows Germans to express their national pride and patriotism without guilt. During the 2006 World Cup, which Germany hosted perfectly, the national flag could be seen everywhere – on buildings, cars, balconies, T-shirts and tattoos. This pride and confidence in the national team is well-merited considering Germany's track record in major tournaments. In fact this became over-confidence in 2006 when Germany chose a part-time trainer who commuted from California to manage their squad. Even then they got to the semi-finals, losing out to the eventual winners. Our German friends say that this was simply good manners, as hosts, letting the guests go first (unlike the unbelievably impolite English in 1966).

Every country has a football club everyone else loves to hate. In Germany it is Bayern Munich. They have dominated German football for as long as most fans can remember, however hard they try to forget. They play in a magnificent, modern stadium which, when lit up at night, looks like a space ship from "Close Encounters of the Third Kind". Fans from other German clubs generally wish this spaceship would lift off, taking the whole of Bayern Munich into a galaxy far, far away.

Germany's most famous player is Franz Beckenbauer. Known as "Kaiser Franz", he led Germany to two World Cup victories, once as captain and once as coach. On the pitch Beckenbauer embodied many of the characteristics of the stereotypical German. He was correct, commanding, highly technical, elegant, unhurried, cool and imperious. In short, he was a brilliant player. His opponents admired him immensely off the field. And hated him intensely on it.

Funny English

Here are 10 of our favourite mistranslations heard from German friends, and the logical explanation of the mistake:

1. **German friend:** "Paul, you must not have coffee. There is tea."
   Paul: "OK. OK. I'll have the tea if you insist."

   "muss nicht" (don't have to) is confused with "must not" (darf nicht)

2. **German friend:** "I work for a really good undertaker."
   Paul: "I thought you were in sales not funerals."

   "Unternehmer" (entrepreneur) is confused with "undertaker" (Leichenbestatter)

3. **German friend:** "Have a look on the backside."
   Paul: "OK. Pull your trousers down!"

   "Rückseite" (back, other side) is confused with "backside" (Hintern)

4. **German friend:** "Remember the figures I gave you last week? Well here are the actual ones."
   Paul: "So what were the figures you gave me last week – lies?"

   "Aktuell" (latest, current) is confused with "actual" (echt)

5. **German friend:** "My chief was really angry with me last week."
   Paul: "Was he on the warpath?"

   "Chef" (boss) is confused with "chief" (Häuptling)

6. **German friend:** "Actually I'm a procurer."
   Paul: "Isn't that illegal in Germany?"

   "Prokurist" (Company Secretary) is confused with "procurer" (Zuhälter)

7. **German friend:** "Can I have a bloody steak?"
   Paul: "And do you want some bloody potatoes too?"

   "blutig" (rare) is confused with "bloody" (verdammt)

8. **German friend:** "Thanks for coming. Good fart."
   Paul: "I didn't do anything. It must have been the dog."

   "Gute Fahrt" (safe journey) is confused with "fart" (Furz)

9. **German friend:** "Let me introduce you to my personal manager."
   Paul: "I didn't know you were a pop star!"

   "Personal" (personnel) is confused with "personal" (persönlich)

10. **German friend:** "A toast. On the ladies!"
    Paul: "Let the orgy begin!"

    "Auf" die Damen ("To" the ladies!) is confused with "On" the ladies!

Sadly we don't have the space to list all the
mistakes we make in German!

Geography

Germany is the biggest country in the European Union and sits firmly in the middle. Most people can draw the outline of their own country quite easily, but with Germany it's like a Rorschach inkblot on the map.

Being in the centre of Europe bordering nine other countries has great advantages: you can easily go shopping for good food in France, go skiing in Austria, sunbathe in Italy, avoid taxes with bank accounts in Luxembourg, yodel in Switzerland and get cheap plumbers from Poland. Sometimes you get the feeling that most Germans want to be somewhere other than in their own country. In the summer they usually are.

Because Germany is so big its geography varies enormously. It extends from the Alps in the south (with cow bells, onion-domed churches and monasteries making extremely strong beer and spirits), to the forests in the west (famous for cuckoo clocks, gateaux or mineral water), the Harz National Park in central Germany (which you usually quickly fly over on the way to Berlin), and to the Baltic and North Sea coasts (where the water temperature motivates most Germans to go swimming in the Mediterranean).

Over 80 million people live in Germany of whom about 2 million are of Turkish origin. The fact is, everyone in Germany considers themselves part of an ethnic minority. The Bavarians see themselves as a separate kingdom (never having fully signed up to the federal system in the first place) with a separate language and culture more similar to their Austrian neighbours to the south. The northern Germans, "Prussians", see themselves as the true Germans. Since they united Germany in the first place (with a bit of arm twisting and military might) they feel a cut above the others. The East Frieslanders and the Saxons feel the others laugh at them, which they do. The Saxons because of their unusual and noticeable accent and the East Frieslanders because – well, because they come from East Friesland.

Berlin is the capital. In fact it's two capital cities. The western half of the city still has an air of decadence from when it was the bastion of

Western civilisation and the spy centre of the world. The eastern half has been almost totally rebuilt, giving it the feeling of a stage set for a Gucci advert.

The new Reichstag was designed by a British architect. (Couldn't they agree on which part of Germany should have the honour of providing the new architect?). The main room is covered by a vast glass construction to symbolize the openness of government. Unfortunately, at the start, this meant that no one could actually hear what the politicians were saying. Many Germans considered this to be the best part of the design. Unfortunately this minor problem has now been corrected. Two cities vie for being considered Germany's second city: Hamburg and Munich. The latter is beautiful, stately, cultured and slightly smug. Hamburg is a port.

German weather is extremely changeable. On any one day it can be cold or warm, sunny or rainy, windy or calm – or any combination. Visitors simply need to pack a huge suitcase for every eventuality. Bavaria has one special weather condition known as the Föhn. This usually occurs when winds blow over the Alps. On the downward slope the winds dry out and heat up. The air clears and you can see the Alps from miles away. It also causes headaches, depression and a feeling of irritation. You can blame all your bad moods on this wind.

Three large rivers run through Germany: the Elbe, the Rhine and the Danube.

The Elbe is a perfect example of the sudden changes in the German weather. In 2002 the Elbe flooded and rose up to 9.5 metres causing widespread devastation. In 2003 it hit a record low level causing most riverboat services to be cancelled. The Rhine is a major artery for goods. You can sit at riverside bars and cafes in Frankfurt or Düsseldorf and watch Dutch barges trying to overtake their German counterparts. It's the industrial version of the Oxford and Cambridge boat race. Each barge has the bargee's car on board. It's similar to those huge Dutch mobile homes that have a car in tow for day trips. The Danube is more famous as a waltz in Austria.

Goethe

Goethe is German culture – all one hundred and forty three volumes of his collected works. (Even Nietzsche only managed just over thirty.)

Goethe's works span poetry, drama, theology, science, literature and philosophy. He was a true polymath and one of the greatest figures in German history. He captured the soul of Germany. His best-known work is his two-part drama "Faust".

But what is not so widely known now about Goethe is that as a young man he was the pop icon of his era. The clothes and traits of characters in his novels and plays were copied by young people everywhere. Another aspect of Goethe that is often missed or, at least skipped over, is his eroticism – both heterosexual and homosexual. It gives his writing a very modern touch.

Goethe is Germany's equivalent to Shakespeare.
And like Shakespeare, not too many people actually read him now.

Handshaking

You are judged by your handshake. Position yourself opposite your partner and follow five very strict rules:

1. It should be very firm –
   no "wet fish" handshakes thank you.

2. It should last two or three shakes –
   no lingering hand holding please.

3. It should be accompanied by direct eye contact –
   no modest dropping of the eyes if you don't mind.

4. It should feel manly –
   even the women.

5. It should be frequent – *each time we meet (sometimes even in the morning and then again in the afternoon).*

Follow these rules and you will be perceived as strong, in control, business-like and – in a nutshell – German.

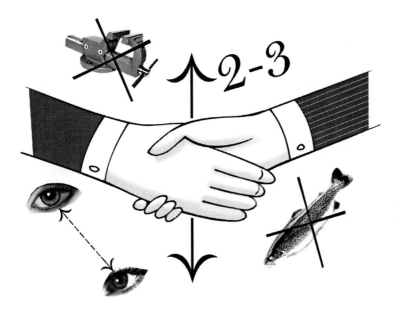

Health

Visitors might believe that Germans are health obsessed or even hypochondriacs. Ask a German friend how they are and you might well get more than you bargained for: "In fact I have a stomach problem and spent most of the night on the toilet." I'm not sure that's what we want to know. A simple "Fine thanks" usually suffices.

Each night on TV you can see men in white coats warning about obesity, gum disease, excess drinking and heart disease. The impression is that most TV ads feature medical personnel in some capacity or other.

German newspapers love health scares. If it's not swine flu or bird flu that gets you, then stress and burn out will. But German health insurance covers just about everything, even covers visits to the spa. "Taking the waters" is an integral part of staying healthy in Germany.

You can swim in them or drink them but preferably not both at the same time. The strange concept of "wellness" has been completely taken to heart. Although the word was originally coined by an American advertising guru, you probably see it more in Germany than in any English speaking country.

As a result, German physicians have a very high status in society. You just don't argue with someone in a white coat. German doctors are known as "Götter in Weiß" or Gods in white. One well-known joke plays on this:

Question: What is the difference between a German doctor and God?

Answer: God doesn't think he's a German doctor.

History

The history of Germany as one nation is a comparatively short one, dating from 1871. In fact, for several reasons, many Germans would prefer it to be an even shorter one, starting in 1948 and the founding of the Federal Republic.

Otto von Bismarck first gained fame as the inventor of Black Velvet, a potent drink made of Russian stout and French champagne. His second claim to fame is as the unifier of Germany.

Prior to 1871 Germany was a patchwork of minor kingdoms, princedoms, duchies, electorates and bishoprics. In order to get these all to work together Bismarck probably needed several stiff drinks. To understand his difficulties you only have to read the story of King Ludwig II of Bavaria (1845 – 1886).

Ludwig was either a brilliant strategic economist or a profligate, self-centred oddball, depending on your perspective. He was certainly eccentric, first falling madly in love with his cousin Sissi (a love that, quite sensibly, was not returned) and then with the composer Wagner.

In between he instigated a castle building spree through which he managed to bankrupt Bavaria. Or maybe he was simply investing for the future and the influx of American tourists looking for the original Disneyland fairy castle.

Ludwig drowned with his doctor in Lake Starnberg whilst being held in captivity by dissatisfied citizens. Some say he was murdered. Others believe he committed suicide. In all likelihood he simply got out of his depth if his history of incompetence is to be believed.

In the 20th century the country's second most famous person is Helmut Kohl, Germany's longest serving chancellor. His greatest claim to fame is the reunification of East and West Germany. This legacy can be seen in the so-called solidarity tax that West Germans still pay to rebuild the East. Mr Kohl unfortunately left office under the cloud of a financial scandal. His successor as leader of the Christian Democratic Union was Angela Merkel, an East German academic and the first woman to lead a major German political party. She was viewed as a temporary replacement until a man could be found. At this time of writing she is well into her second decade as Mr Kohl's temporary replacement.

Humour

There is none. Or that's what you are led to believe. No, there is a great deal of humour in the German way of life. It's just different from what you may think is funny. First of all, humour is not used in your working life to jolly the boss along, to poke fun at your own mistakes or to entertain your colleagues in meetings. This is seen as not taking the business seriously. For example, most British business presentations start with a joke, often a self-deprecating story. Most German business presentations start with a long and detailed agenda for the discussion. No one uses ironic humour in meetings. This is misinterpreted as mocking sarcasm!

German humour is a much more serious business. Time needs be set aside for humorous activities. Humour needs to take place in the appropriate place and at an appropriate time. Like the "Karneval" celebrations in Cologne, where you are officially asked to be funny for several weeks on end. For most non-Germans, sitting through a Karneval's humorous celebratory evening is at best incomprehensible, and at worst slightly unnerving.

German humour is traditionally very harsh, dark, acidic and scatological. It stems from the cabaret of the 1930s. The problem is that type of humour does not translate very well. When such jokes are told and translated, they frequently have to be explained. The explanation always takes more time than the joke itself. By the time you have understood the explanation, you've forgotten the joke. Germans don't do self-deprecating humour. There is nearly always a butt to the joke such as the idiotic Austrian (if you are German), the uptight Prussian (if you are from Bavaria), the bucolic Bavarian (if you are from northern Germany) and the tight-fisted Swabian (if you are from anywhere else). Perhaps this is because of a lack of national self-esteem, but certainly making fun of yourself is not seen as particularly amusing or as a sign of self-confidence like in the United States or UK.

We do have one type of humour in common: Murphy's Law, "If anything can go wrong, it will." It seems that all of us find amusing the idea that life is full of things that go wrong, and that there is nothing we can do about it. Most of our German friends take it a step further: "If nothing went wrong, it probably would have been better if it had."

Hunting

The patron saint of hunters is St Hubertus and he is especially revered in Germany. He was a dedicated hunter until one Good Friday. While everyone else was in church, Hubertus was out stag hunting in the Ardennes. He tracked down a magnificent stag and just as he was about to loosen his arrow, the stag turned to face him. Between its antlers was a glowing cross. A voice then said, "Hubert, unless thou turnest to the Lord and leadest a holy life, thou shalt quickly go down into hell". This would be enough to put anyone off their hunting. Hubertus was no exception. He gave it up and became bishop of Maastricht instead.

Hunting is extremely popular in Germany. Hunters are respected members of the community, belonging to hunting clubs and teams with special traditions which are handed down from one generation of hunters to the next. They are easy to recognise by their green Robin Hood style hats decorated with feathers, which they love to wear when not hunting. You will meet them everywhere. One place you will be sure to find them is at the German Museum of Hunting and Fishing in Munich. There are green Robin Hood hats everywhere there and the largest display of antlers you will see in your life.

Hunting is like everything in Germany; it has rules. You must pass an exam to get a hunting licence. And it's no easy exam. There is a high failure rate. It's a long course involving the theory and practice of shooting, weaponry, wild life conservation and good hunting etiquette. The final certificate has the cachet of a university degree. It's hunting with an intellectual edge!

Most of Germany's half a million hunters have yet to meet Hubertus' stag. So they continue to hunt. They often warm themselves up during the long hours of waiting with a sip of Jägermeister bitters. They can see the stag's head with a glowing cross between the antlers on the label. It's just a gentle reminder of what could happen to them.

Instant German

German is (almost) English. There is a common myth that German is a difficult language to learn. Untrue! Look at any German newspaper and you'll have the strange feeling you're reading a strange English dialect.

Because German and English share Anglo-Saxon roots and because German is an avid importer of English words, about 40% of German vocabulary is recognizably English. The percentage would have been much higher if King Harold hadn't got a French arrow in his eye at the Battle of Hastings in 1066 (and thus paving the way for the "latinization" of English).

Of the 1000 most commonly used English words, 65% have equivalents in German. For example, the German words Finger, Hand, Arm, are identical. Haar, Lippen, Nase (hair, lips, nose) are close enough to be immediately recognizable; and Schulter, Herz, and Knie (shoulder, heart, and knee) yield to a little bit of detective work.

Enno von Loewenstern wrote an amusing German article for The New York Times which was largely understood by English readers. A sample:

Unser Way of Life im Media Business ist hart, da muss man ein tougher Kerl sein. Morgens Warm-up und Stretching, dann ein Teller Corn Flakes und ein Soft Drink oder Darjeeling Tea, dann in das Office - und schon Brunch mit den Top-Leuten,....

Unfortunately for German language purists, speaking English with a German accent is now almost sufficient to make yourself understood anywhere in the country.

Kindergarten German

You already know Kindergarten, Rucksack, Schnitzel, Wanderlust ... and dozens of other German words, so why not use them? Pepper your German with such imports, and don't worry about pronunciation.

Mistakes and a foreign accent are the keys to success in German. In contrast to our French cousins, the Germans are very supportive of foreigners trying to speak their language, however imperfectly.

You can go a long way with these 99 German words which are already firmly embedded in English:

Achtung!, Alzheimer, Angst, Auf Wiedersehen, Apfelstrudel, Aspirin, Autobahn, Blitzkrieg, Bratwurst, Christkindl, Dachshund, Delikatessen, Diesel, Dirndl, Dobermann Pinscher, Doppelgänger, Doppler effect, Dummkopf, Edelweiss, Ersatz, Fahrenheit, Fahrvergnügen, Fest, Flak, Frau, Fräulein, Frankfurter, Führer, Gasthaus, Gauss, Gemütlichkeit, Gestalt, Gesundheit, Gewürztraminer, Glockenspiel, Götterdämmerung, Hamburger, Hamster, Hertz, Hinterland, Kaffeeklatsch, Kaiser, kaputt, Kindergarten, Kitsch, Kobalt, Konzertmeister, Lebensraum, Leberwurst, Lederhosen, Liebfrauenmilch, Leitmotiv, Lied, Leberwurst, Masochismus, Neanderthal, Nickel, Ostpolitik, Panzer, Poltergeist, Putsch, Quartz, Realpolitik, Reich, Rottweiler, Rucksack, Sauerbraten, Sauerkraut, Schadenfreude, Schnapps, Schnauzer, Schnitzel, Schweinehund, Strudel, Übermensch, verboten, Volkswagen, Vorsprung durch Technik, Waltz, Waldsterben, Wanderlust, Weltanschauung, Weltschmerz, Wienerschnitzel, wunderbar, Wunderkind, Zeitgeist, Zeppelin, Zink.

By the way, those funny letters with the two dots are easier than they look. Remember three tips and you can start reading Goethe immediately!

☞ ä is pronounced just like the first letter of the alphabet "A",

☞ for ö just say the "ur" in murder,

☞ and ü just say the "oo" in moon

Those Gargantuan German Words

Words that roll so easily off the German tongue, scare the hell out of foreigners. How many would-be German speakers are willing to risk:

Geschwindigkeitsbegrenzung (speed limit), Verantwortungszuständig-keiten (areas of responsibility), or Rindfleischetikettierungsüberwa-chungsaufgabenübertragungsgesetz (beef labeling regulation & delegation of supervision law)?

And how we marvel at the fact that any German schoolchild can rattle off: "Donaudampfschifffahrtselektrizitätenhauptbetriebswerkbau-unterbeamtengesellschaft" (The Association for subordinate officials of the head office management of the Danube steamboat electrical services).

But don't be misled. German only appears difficult. The moment one grasps the principle of bite-sized chunks, German suddenly becomes digestable. Say this and be proud:

Do-nau dampf-schif-fahrts e-lek-tri-zi-tä-ten haupt-be-triebs-werk-bau unter-be-amt-en ge-sell-schaft.

Which just goes to show that even German yields to salami tactics.

Instant German Conversation

Speak German instantly by speaking weird English. We used to wonder why Germans used so much bad language until we learned that damit means "therefore" and not "Damn it!" Or that fahrt means "journey" and has nothing to do with farting!

We also wondered why the English trio "Nick, Sue, Duncan" are so popular in Germany, until we realized that it is phonetically identical to Nichts zu danken! which means "Don't mention it" or "The pleasure is mine." So whenever a German thanks you for your help, simply say "Nick, Sue, Duncan" for a perfect German answer.

The following English conversation looks rather strange, but it's easy to read, and to Germans it's music to the ears.

In a bar, somewhere in Germany:

B: **End shoe, tea gun, sea!**
    (Excuse me!)
    Ken Ann, veer Huns?
    (Don't I know you from somewhere?)

F: **Itch bin nicked, sicker.**
    (I'm really not sure.)

B: **Bitter, fair cyan, mine comb midges, hack scent,...**
    Itch bin, house lander.
    (Please excuse my poor pronunciation,..
    but I'm not from these parts.)

F. **Fighter so, itch Lee bear, diner house, spray care. Fair click!**
    (Do continue, I just love your way of speaking. Really!)

B. **Mine armour heist Bob, gun itch dish,**
   iron lard hen, Sue iron, get rank?
   (I'm Bob. May I invite you for a drink?)

F. **Sicker Bob. Itch bin Franz. Hick leaper vice vine.**
   (Certainly Bob. I'm Franz. I'll go for a white wine.)

B. **Probe ear mull, teaser flusher.**
   (Try this bottle.)

F. **Zoom vole!**
   (Cheers!)

B. **Alf Dick!**
   (To your good health!)

F. **Mmm... smacked wonder bar, harbour dare flusher, hissed fussed leer.**
   (Mmmm... this tastes very good, but the bottle's almost empty.)

B. **Itch roof, dare kiln air.**
   (I will summon the waiter.)
   Hair robe air!
   (Waiter!)

B. **Bring gun, seance bitter, knock iron air, flusher. Harbour colt.**
   (Kindly bring us another bottle, nicely chilled.)

W. **Sell fairs tend lick, mine hair!**
   (Certainly, Sir!)

B. **So Franz, fair art hen, seem ear. Fuss muck hen sea, bay roof, lick?**
   (So Franz, be so kind as to tell me. What do you?)

F. **Itch bin under you knee. Itch under Rick dare, hang list tick.**
   (I am a professor of English at the university.)

B. **House get sigh net! Lass soons, iron piss yen, English ray den.**
   (Excellent! Let us then exchange a few words in my own tongue.)

Learn these instant phrases and try them out on your German
friends and colleagues. You (and they) will be amazed!

Inventions

Einstein is probably the most famous German scientist and mathematician, but there are plenty more.

Did you know that aspirin was a German invention? If you didn't, that's probably one headache cleared up. Mind you, the same company that cured our hangovers also introduced heroin to the world as a cough suppressant and as a way to stop smoking!

Germany also gave us sports shoes and trainers. Maybe this is why drug dealers are well-known for wearing the latest models.

Two very practical German inventions are the coffee filter and the MP3 player. One prevents the coffee grounds from disturbing your taste. The other prevents your taste in music from disturbing everyone else.

Two very different modes of transport were German inventions. The automobile changed the world and provides the means for poor, desert countries to become rich and powerful. But then we have the Zeppelin. How could anyone think that a huge balloon filled with combustible gases was a safe way to cross the Atlantic?

Other German inventions include the printing press, without which our tabloid newspapers could not be printed. Oh well, scientific advances do have some negative side-effects.

Mr Heinz of Heinz Tomato Ketchup was German. He moved to the United States and probably invented his famous ketchup so that he could eat the fast food he encountered.

And did you know the Christmas tree also originated in Germany? Based on pagan rituals it first became popular in the 16th century. It is rumoured that Martin Luther had the idea of adding candles and some other decorations, but that sounds a bit too frivolous for him. It was taken to Britain by the Hanoverian monarchs and then spread to the United States where tree decoration really took off. In America you can hardly see the tree for the lights.

We should be grateful to our German inventors, especially two German gynaecologists who invented the first scientific pregnancy tests. They have helped calm the nerves of countless men.

Italy

The majority of Germans love Italy and all things Italian. Ask your average German their favourite cuisine and they invariably answer "Italian".

Ask your average German their favourite holiday resort and they answer "Lake Garda or Tuscany." Ask your average German man where you can find the most beautiful girls and he answers "Italy".

So why the love affair with Italy? It's not only the pizza, pasta, and wine. Maybe it's because Italy is easy to visit and it's the nearest country with a totally different culture. Germans admire Italians for such traits as:

∞ They are laid back about life and living.

∞ They ignore rules and regulations.

∞ They don't pay their taxes.

∞ They vote for scandalous politicians.

- They are outgoing, and friendly.

- Their language sounds like music.

- They show their feelings with passion.

- They love to laugh out loud.

And to cap it all Italians live in a country with beautiful beaches and long hot summers. Opposites attract they say.

Mittelstand

The majority of German companies are small or medium sized family run businesses (the Mittelstand). There is usually a benevolent, all-powerful father figure at the head. This is the founder, the founder's son, his grandson or great grandson. He knows his company, its products and his workforce inside out. He is highly respected by his workers because he has done his time on the workshop floor, occasionally joins the boys at the local beer hall "Stammtisch" and knows all the tricks of the trade. Without him, Germany and the Germans would not be working.

Mobile Phones

In Germany the mobile phone is called a "Handy." Most Germans assume they have simply borrowed the English word for mobile phone. They are surprised to hear that "a handy" is English baby-talk for the thing at the end of your arm.

Money

Germany suffered from hyperinflation in the 1920s and 1940s. Stories of people taking wheelbarrows of paper money to the shops are common. Everyone lost their hard-earned savings. And this experience has coloured the German attitude to money and wealth.

Having personal wealth based on a solid currency means security. This explains the soul-searching that went on in Germany when the old, strong, dependable German Mark was replaced by the untried and untested Euro. (Can the French really help us run a central bank?)

It might also explain why Germany was slow in adopting the use of credit cards. Even now, many German restaurants, bars and shops only accept cash. Bank notes are real money. Credit cards are just a form of plastic IOU.

This might also explain why Germans are the world champions when it comes to saving money. Each high street has several local savings banks with advertisements designed to make you worried about the size of your retirement pension from the day you leave school.

Having enough money is important and there is nothing wrong with showing your wealth as long as you do it in a low-key way. You don't speak about money – you have it! If you have worked hard and made money, then your clothes, shoes, cars, houses, jewellery, watches and your wives should reflect this. But what you definitely mustn't do is talk about it. Talking salaries is taboo. Never ask a German business partner, "What do you make?" It could be the end of a beautiful friendship (and a great business opportunity).

But maybe Goethe had the right attitude to all of this, combining the German need for financial prudence with the philosopher's approach to living a meaningful life. He wrote, "Many people take no care of their money till they come nearly to the end of it, and others do just the same with their time."

Music

Internationally acclaimed pop stars:
There aren't any.

Internationally acclaimed classical musicians:
There are too many to mention.

After all, Germany is the land of Bach, Beethoven, Bruckner, Gluck, Mahler, F. Mendelssohn-Bartholdy, Pachelbel, Schumann, Stockhausen, R. Strauss, Telemann, Wagner, Weber and the mighty Berlin Philharmonic.

Even that great British composer, Handel, was German.

Names

At Hanover Trade Fair a Japanese businessman is met on a stand by three Germans. Two of them happen to be called Schmidt. The first Mr Schmidt shakes the hand of the Japanese and says, "Schmidt." The second does the same, "Schmidt." The Japanese turns to Mr Frank, the third German and says, "Schmidt, Schmidt" – as a greeting.

In Germany people often use their family name as a kind of greeting and then expect to be called by it. But many German family names are difficult to pronounce for English speakers. Being confronted by a Mr Homrighausen, a Mrs Eicheberger and a Doctor Bachmeier can be quite worrying for them.

Anglo-Saxons try to go to first names as soon as possible. Franz, Eva and Holger are certainly much easier to pronounce than the family names. In fact most Germans are aware of the problem their names can cause internationally. They are quite prepared to use first names with English speakers. But this can lead to a strange situation. People who have known each other for ten years still call each other "Mr Homrighausen" or "Mrs Eicheberger". But for the native English speaker they met ten minutes ago, it's "John" or "Mary".

Nudity

If you are of a nervous, shy or delicate disposition do not go into the sauna in a German spa hotel. You will meet totally naked people of both sexes, all age groups and all shapes and sizes. It is not a sight for the faint-hearted British who wouldn't dream of entering a sauna without a swimsuit. One rather prudish British acquaintance quickly left a sauna when confronted with this sight. Friends asked him why he had left in such a hurry. Was it because he was embarrassed? "No", he replied. "I was afraid!"

There is certainly a different attitude to the naked body in Germany compared with many other cultures. Frei-Körper-Kultur (literally Free Body Culture or nudism) is an accepted part of the German way of life. You find FKK beaches or sun-bathing areas in many places (the nude sun-bathing area in the English Garden in Munich has actually become a very popular tourist attraction!). This pragmatic, matter-of-fact approach is quite refreshing but sometimes surprising.

On a crowded beach on Lanzarote, two naked people pose on a small headland looking out to sea, each with one hand resting on the other's buttocks. They are in full view of about five hundred fully dressed or swimsuit clad holiday makers who whisper: "They must be German". They are.

Oktoberfest

This is the most famous beer festival in the world. The Oktoberfest is held in Munich and takes place over two and a half weeks - mainly in September! This is a case of German punctuality being taken to extremes. To give you some idea of what happens, here are a few rough statistics:

- ∞ 7 million litres of beer are drunk
- ∞ 100,000 litres of wine are tippled
- ∞ Half a million chickens are eaten

- 100 oxen are consumed

- 60,000 pork knuckles are put away

- 160,000 sausages are munched

This food and drink are served in huge tents, usually by buxom ladies renowned for their ability to carry several litres of beer at once and for their low cut traditional dresses that reveal plenty of cleavage.

The patrons are entertained by "oompah" bands and by taking turns dancing on (and occasionally falling off) the tables. In 2004 the police had to be called in to regulate the traffic to and from the toilets. This situation has improved since the use of mobile phones was banned in the toilet stalls. The Oktoberfest funfair offers something for everyone depending on your urge for adventure. But the thought of eating all that food, drinking all that beer and then going on a roller coaster is not one for the squeamish.

Book your accommodation early. All the hotels, hostels and campsites are packed to overflowing. But here's a tip. Why not just advertise in the local paper as a house sitter for all those citizens who flee Munich while the Oktoberfest is on?

Ostalgie

There has been a wave of nostalgia for the DDR (The old East German communist state). Goodness only knows why. It was a pretty awful part of German history with state control, drab concrete high-rises, pollution, oppression and depression.

But in the east there is a nostalgia for full, state sponsored employment and cradle-to-grave social security. In the west there is a sentimental nostalgia for Trabant cars (which couldn't overtake a fit cyclist and which leave a street-length plume of smoke from the exhaust), songs of the Young Pioneers (a sort of militant Boy Scout movement), Spreewaldgurken (pickled cucumbers which taste like no cucumber you've ever eaten) and Florena hand cream (tried and tested on the hands of millions of female DDR factory workers). There are even plans for a DDR theme park. Part of this nostalgia has been created or at least reflected in such excellent films as "Sun Alley" and "Goodbye Lenin." They evoke everything nostalgic about the DDR. But if you need an antidote to this "Ostalgie" phenomenon, watch the Oscar winning film "The Lives of Others". No one is nostalgic for the Stasi.

Perfection

"It's not what you do, it's the way that you do it." These words to an old song capture the German mentality. You can also add the words of the old saying, "If a thing is worth doing, it's worth doing well."

In the UK you might well see a motorcyclist on a BMW bike, wearing a scuffed Harley Davidson leather jacket, a Moto-Guzzi t-shirt, old jeans rather than leathers, a scratched and battered crash helmet and a pair of gloves that look as if they were used by Second World War despatch riders. In Germany the equivalent motorcyclist would be immaculately dressed in the total BMW outfit, with matching everything. And you can translate this to any walk of life. Skiers look as though they have slalomed out of the advert for a ski resort. Cyclists all look as though they took part in the last Tour de France. Golfers are all seemingly on the professional tour with scratch handicaps. Even joggers look as if they are just about to compete in the next Olympic marathon. This demand for perfection is noticeable in business too. Reports should cover every detail. Presentations should show every argument. Products should be engineered to be faultless. Staff make no mistakes. This certainly gives Germans a reputation for reliability and quality. And makes the rest of us feel somewhat inadequate.

Punctuality

People are not really obsessed by punctuality in Germany. If you turn up to a meeting 30 seconds late, you may well be forgiven.

Religion

Religion in Germany can be summarised by the following quotes:

1. **"Wir sind Papst"**
   (literally "We are Pope")
   Headline in the newspaper Bild Zeitung on the election of the German cardinal Josef Ratzinger as Pope Benedict XVI in 2005.

2. **"I am much freer now that I am certain the pope is the Antichrist."**
   Martin Luther (16th Century German initiator of the Protestant reformation)

3. **"God is dead."**
   Friedrich Nietzsche
   (19th century German philosopher)

About a third of the German population subscribes to each one of these three faiths, with Catholics concentrated in the south, Protestants in the north, and Unbelievers pretty well everywhere.

Rubbish

Germans know their rubbish. They are expert rubbish sorters. They know which piece of rubbish goes into which receptacle, based on the national master plan. Big skips for paper can be found everywhere. Not cardboard. Not milk cartons. Not juice containers. Paper. If you do put your cardboard wrapping from your parcels in there, take off the address label first. Otherwise you face a hefty fine. The same goes for glass. Don't put your brown bottles in the green bottle skip! And remember, you can only use these skips between certain hours of the day. If you commute long distances you are never home when it's legal to throw away your bottles. Either you take your bottles to work with you. Or you stop drinking.

In some places you save all your packaging material in a special yellow sack. This is only collected once a month. Shopaholics have to make several trips to the recycling depot in between times. There are also special green or brown dustbins for biodegradable waste – mainly food, more food and yet more food again.

Finally you have the black dustbin for the remainder such as the broken china, smashed up toys and condoms. (You haven't been flushing them down the loo have you? If they block the plumbing in your block of flats you will have to emigrate). Your local council will take away old fridges, TV sets and used paint pots. Add the cost of this to your budget for new equipment or redecorating the bathroom. Having said all this, it generally works! Germany is one of the leading countries in the world in household waste management. Their streets, roads, and autobahns are among the cleanest in Europe. So when talking about protecting the environment, you certainly can't rubbish the Germans!

Rules

Rules in Germany are not made to be broken. And there are plenty of them. If you live in Germany we can almost guarantee the following:

- ☞ You will not be kept awake after 11 pm by someone showering at length in the flat above yours or by singing in the bath.

- ☞ You will not be woken up by the sound of empty beer and wine bottles crashing into the dustbin between 10 pm and 7 am. In fact you will not be woken up by much happening after 10 pm.

- ☞ Your Sunday afternoon nap will not be disturbed by your neighbour mowing his lawn. If he doesn't cut it at all, you can report him to the authorities.

- ☞ You will not run over pedestrians crossing against red lights or walking in cycle lanes even late at night when yours is the only car or cycle in sight. If any of these things do happen to you then the people concerned are either foreigners, tourists or both.

It's best to assume that most things are forbidden unless you have documentary proof of the opposite. But Germany is changing. We occasionally use a hotel in Schliersee where they once had a board at the entrance to their indoor pool listing twenty nine rules for using the facility. The last time we were there it had been replaced by a board listing only twenty one.

Sauerkraut

Sour cabbage – yuck! You take a cabbage, finely shred it and then ferment it with salt. The lactic acid bacteria present in the cabbage go to work to give it its distinctive sour taste. So it's actually fermented sour cabbage! Even worse!

The truth is, it tastes a lot better than its name or the preparation process implies. Here are some little-known facts about sauerkraut:

1. It has more anti-cancer agents than raw vegetables. That's good news. No more broccoli!

2. Captain James Cook always had barrels of sauerkraut on his ship during his long voyages of discovery to prevent scurvy.

3. There is an annual "Krautfest" held in the small town Leinfelden-Echterdingen that attracts over 40,000 visitors. (We're not sure it's a good idea to have 40,000 people eating sauerkraut in a small area. Hopefully it's mainly outdoors.)

4. One of Elvis's favourite dishes was sauerkraut with bacon and mashed potatoes. But then his other favourite dishes included fried squirrel and deep-fried peanut butter and banana sandwiches!

5. During World War 1 the word sauerkraut was banned in the USA. No-one would buy products that sounded German Sauerkraut was renamed "liberty cabbage."

Perhaps the most surprising and important fact is this: Nutritionist Leyla Kazinic Kreho claims that sauerkraut is an even more powerful aphrodisiac than Viagra!! So why is the German birth rate declining? Eat more sauerkraut!

Schiller

In 2008 Schiller was voted the second most influential European playwright after Shakespeare (admittedly by the audience of the Franco-German TV channel Arte). His revolutionary play "The

Robbers" was a sensation at the time, eventually leading to an offer of honorary citizenship of the French Republic by the Jacobins (an honour he rejected because he was disgusted by the on-going executions). He became friends with Goethe and together they created the Weimar Classicism movement.

Like most poet-playwrights he died of tuberculosis. After he died in 1805, Schiller's body was interred in the Weimar Ducal Vault. Tests carried out in 2008 on the skull of Schiller's skeleton proved it was not his head. So where is it? Who has it? And what would anyone want to do with it? As Schiller himself wrote, "Against stupidity the gods themselves contend in vain."

Skiing

Many Germans love to go skiing. They have some great alpine ski resorts (although not quite as many as their Austrian and Swiss neighbours). They have a long tradition of winter sports (although not quite as long as their Austrian and Swiss neighbours). They have produced many great ski champions (although not quite as many as their Austrian and Swiss neighbours).

Many Germans love to go skiing in Austria and Switzerland.

Small Talk

There is none. Especially in business. For many Germans small talk is just that; small! It's a waste of time, and time is money. As the German saying goes, "Erst die Arbeit dann das Vergnugen" (Work before pleasure).

If you attend a business meeting in Germany, don't be surprised if your hosts greet you, say one or two words about your trip and then dive straight into the subject at hand. It's not that they are being unfriendly. It's not that they are being impolite. It's not that they are not interested in you. They just feel uncomfortable with the "small" in small talk.

Stammtisch

Most pubs, bars or beer halls have a "Stammtisch." This is a table reserved for regular customers. It's usually clearly shown with a brass plaque or wooden marker. This is where the regulars sit and chat, play cards and think they get preferential service.

Two things to remember about the "Stammtisch":

1. If you are invited to join your local pub's "Stammtisch" it means you have been accepted as "one of us".

2. If you sit there uninvited...

Television

German television is well-known for two things:

1. **Dubbing**
   All foreign language programmes are dubbed in German. So you will have the dubious pleasure of watching your favourite soap character speaking like Angela Merkel or of Harrison Ford sounding like Gerhard Schroeder. "Synchronisation" or dubbing gives films the character of early talkies when the sound and lip movements did not quite match up. It also provides a lot of work for mediocre actors. The voice-over industry is big. Actors

become known for their voices and often specialise in dubbing well-known Hollywood stars. Gert-Günther Hoffman was James Bond until he died in 1997. Since then five different voices have been used. Joachim Tennstedt has managed to be Kevin Costner, Billy Crystal, Mel Gibson and C3PO – no mean feat. There is an educational argument for releasing films in their original language with sub-titles like in The Netherlands and Scandinavia. Kids get used to hearing English and this has a positive spin-off at school. There are two arguments against this. English teachers (and parents) don't want children talking like Eddie Murphy or Eminem. Second, the voice-over industry would collapse, putting thousands of people out of work and increasing the costs of the social benefits system.

2. **Talk shows**

Every evening on several channels you can tune in to talk shows. These are interminably long discussions with several very long-winded, opinionated guests talking about things that most viewers find boring, in a way that indicates that the speakers find it pretty boring too. You get the feeling that no one's heart is really in this type of programme but that it has to be done to show that the channel takes its government funding seriously.

Tipping

Americans are expected to leave a 15% tip for the waiter. In most other countries it's 10%. In German restaurants or taxis you simply have to round the bill up. This rarely exceeds 5%. So why is Germany different? Our German friends usually try to tell us that it's due to complicated German tax regulations. We think it a lot simpler. Most Germans do not expect good service, so why tip? Up until quite recently service was not a word one connected with waiters, taxi drivers or shop assistants. Efficiency yes, service no. Gradually this began to change. But then the Wall came down. Suddenly there was an influx of low-paid service staff from the East. They were accustomed to a system where service was a class enemy. You considered yourself lucky if there was any service to buy at all. Germans traditionally expect bad service and the tips reflect this.

But again, Germany is changing. Nowadays you meet personable waitresses, cheerful cab drivers and helpful hotel staff. And sadly, they just don't get the tips they deserve.

Toilet Attendants

In many parts of Germany public toilets are run, cleaned and supervised by a specially appointed attendant. This is usually, but not always, a large, fierce, middle-aged lady of Eastern European extraction who sits outside the loos with a plate on which you are expected to leave a tip. And woe betide you if you don't! The plate might be rattled at you alarmingly. A gruff cough will remind you of your tipping duties. Dirty looks will follow you if you fail to leave the obligatory 50 cents. And her brother / cousin / husband / minder will casually slow down your exit by chatting to another brother / cousin / husband / minder across the entrance. It's almost mafiaesque.

So be warned. Keep that 50 cent coin handy at all times. You never know when you might have to run the gauntlet of the German toilet attendant.

Toilets

Many visitors to Germany are curious about the shape of some German toilet bowls. There is a kind of shelf in the bowl from which everything is then flushed. What on earth can it be for you might ask? Is it for a more even distribution of the waste so the pipes don't get blocked? Is it to prevent your backside being splashed if waste drops directly into the water?

Is it some kind of toilet and douche all in one?

No. It's simply there to allow you to examine everything for signs of ill health. For most people from other cultures this is not a pretty thought. But for many health conscious Germans it's an important part of the daily ritual like brushing your teeth (just as long as you don't get the two mixed up, we say).

Tourism

Spain would be bankrupt without German tourists. You get the impression that Germany invented the mass escape to the sun and still sustains it. Other tourists are simply amateurs compared to their German counterparts. Wherever you go on holiday in the world, you can see groups of serious-looking people in shorts and with backpacks and alpine walking sticks being harangued at length by a tour guide in German.

German tourists are especially renowned for two things;

1. **Following the guidebook.**
   As a German tourist you have to have studied your guidebook in great detail. Just think if you went home and Schmidt next door asks if you ate at that incredible seafood restaurant just down on the harbour, which is in all the guidebooks – and you haven't. To make it worse you missed the beautiful monastery in the mountains too!

2. Marking territory with towels

Everybody does this now. But it is a direct response to German tourists who have long reserved sun-loungers near the pool with their towels. Some tourists take this very seriously, getting up at 5 am to lay out the towels before going back to bed again. If you really want to cause confusion, go out to the pool area during breakfast and change the towels around. Then sit in the shade somewhere and watch what happens.

Trains

Travelling by train in Germany is generally a pleasure. You make your connections and you arrive where you should, when you should. The train conductors are knowledgeable, helpful, and friendly and speak excellent English. The high-speed ICE trains are comfortable and quick.

Three small drawbacks to travelling by train:

- ↪ Make sure that you are not sitting in a pre-booked seat. If so, you might be subjected to self-righteous indignation from the seat holder or a telling off from the otherwise pleasant conductor.

- ↪ When offering to help some little old lady with her luggage, you might need to explain that you do not want payment and that you are not a thief.

- ↪ Stations are incredibly busy on Sundays. It's not that everyone is travelling somewhere. It's just locals doing their shopping because station shops are the only ones open (together with petrol stations and airports). So expect to be jostled by other little old ladies with shopping trolleys and families enjoying window shopping and a bratwurst.

If you are British and travelling on a German train with traditional compartments, remember to greet your fellow travellers on entering and don't forget to say "Auf Wiedersehen" when leaving. This is customary and polite in Germany, but not in the UK where you never speak to fellow passengers. (The only exception to this is when the train is late. Then you can talk to each other in order to have a mutual complaining session. This means the no-talking rule is frequently broken in the UK because British trains are usually late.)

Wagner

Two famous Germans fell in love with Richard Wagner and his music: the eccentric King Ludwig II of Bavaria and Adolf Hitler, neither of whose judgement you would necessarily trust. Wagner was nevertheless a huge influence on the development of modern European classical music. Poor Wagner was in debt for most of his life and had to be periodically rescued by Ludwig. But it didn't prevent him from creating some of the most expensive productions in opera history.

His most famous operas are the Ring cycle. These four operas took him over thirty years to complete and take fifteen hours to watch. If you can get tickets, you can do that at Bayreuth Festspielhaus, which was custom built for Wagner (courtesy of his patron Ludwig). Lucky Richard. The music in the Ring cycle is amazing. Each opera is one continuous piece with no breaks. You have no time to take a breath (or go to the loo). Wagner called them "music dramas" rather than operas.

Drama is an appropriate word to describe Wagner's own life story. His first marriage was a disaster with his wife running off with an army officer and then returning. He went into exile to escape creditors in Riga, became a revolutionary in Saxony, befriended the mad anarchist Bakunin, fled to Zurich, fell in love with a married woman, moved to Munich under Ludwig's patronage, fell in love with a disapproving Franz Liszt's illegitimate daughter, was forced to leave Munich by people afraid of his influence over the king and finally settled in Bayreuth and built the opera house of his dreams.

Maybe he should have written an opera based on that.

Wine

German wine has a poor reputation in the UK. As the British began to change their drinking styles in the 50s and 60s, the market was flooded with sweet German white wine like Liebfraumilch. Originally a fairly classy hock, Liebfraumilch was mass-produced. The cheap export version has a sugar content that sticks your lips together as you drink it and a taste that reminds you of boiled sweets from your childhood. Wine connoisseurs in many countries try to avoid it. This perception of German white wines as cheap and sweet has been hard to change.

In fact Germany produces many superb wines, most notably the top quality Rieslings. We love the crisp, tangy taste of a good dry Riesling, served at exactly 7.7 degrees celcius. Even some of the German red wines have become internationally renowned. Our favourite is a good quality Spätburgunder (Pinot Noir).

But bad reputations stick. You have to search high and low in most British wine merchants to find good quality German wines amongst the thousands of French, Italian, Spanish and New World varieties. There are usually more wines from Chile on display than German ones!

So come on Germany. Don't keep all your good wines for yourselves like the Swiss. Let the world know how good your wines and send us some real Liebfraumilch.

Work and Pleasure

"Dienst ist Dienst und Schnapps ist Schnapps".

You should clearly separate work from pleasure. You do your duty diligently and with due care and attention. You work hard. You treat your colleagues seriously and with respect. You rarely smile and joke with them during meetings. You do not share information about your private lives. You are Herr or Frau Schmidt.

Duty is duty.

Then you leave work on a Friday evening. You might join your old school friends at the Stammtisch for a couple of drinks. You might meet up with your partner's family for dinner. You will take the kids to their various sporting activities on Saturday. You will work in the garden and chat to the neighbours. You will smile, laugh and joke with all of them. You will not meet any of your work colleagues. You are Franz or Claudia.

Schnapps is Schnapps.

World War II

"Don't mention the war!"

In the British comedy "Fawlty Towers", John Cleese plays a hotel owner who repeatedly tells himself "Don't mention the war" when he has to deal with German guests. Of course, everything he does or says accidentally refers to World War II.

But is this piece of advice actually true when visiting Germany? Not any more. For many, especially younger Germans, talking about recent history is not taboo. You can certainly discuss it with your German friends.

Perhaps we should thank Franz Josef Strauss for starting to break the ice. During the cold war, and as Minister President of Bavaria, Strauss made a historic trip to Russia.

69

When asked by Leonid Brezhnev if he had ever before been to Moscow, Strauss answered "No, I only got as far as Stalingrad!" After an excruciating silence during which Strauss's aides wished they had stayed in Munich, Brezhnev smiled, the meeting was saved. Strauss returned home a hero. So even if a sense of guilt still lingers, you can mention the war. But be prepared for an interesting, in-depth discussion for several hours over several beers. By the third one you might be up to 1940. And you soon recognise that one of the main results has been to make post-war Germany one of the strongest democracies in the world.

Xmas

The Germans invented Christmas – or at least most of the traditions surrounding it. The Christmas tree is a German invention. So are Christmas carols, Christmas cards, Christmas presents, and Christmas decorations.

And they take Christmas very seriously. You know that Christmas is taken seriously when there are towns like Rothenburg which have a year-round Christmas shop selling everything you could possibly want to decorate your home and tree. The shop does a roaring trade in July as well as November.

↪ You know that Christmas is taken seriously when the celebrations start at the beginning of December and go through to January 6.

↪ You know that Christmas is taken seriously when there is so much special Christmas food on offer.

↪ You know that Christmas is taken seriously when the churches are packed to overflowing.

↪ You know that Christmas is being taken seriously when the whole country closes completely for three days.

Yes, the Germans take Christmas very seriously. And that's why it's so enjoyable.

Zeitgeist

The German Romanticist movement created the concept of "The spirit of the age". They viewed each era as having a specific outlook, which is reflected in its literature, philosophy and attitudes. Hegel made the idea popular and acceptable.

So what is the zeitgeist of present day Germany?

One part of the answer you can find in part 2 of this book. The results of the survey "The Real Truth about the Germans" provide insights into how Germans see the zeitgeist of modern Germany.

For the other part of the answer, go and stay a while in this incredible country and experience the German zeitgeist for yourself. It's guaranteed to be a fascinating and rewarding experience.

Part 2 — Survey results

THE REAL TRUTH ABOUT THE GERMANS

A survey to discover how Germans see Germans

Fair or not, the global stereotype of the serious, efficient, Mercedes-driving German is still a strong perception in other countries. Do Germans also see themselves this way? In September 2009, over 2,000 German speakers participated in an online survey to answer the question:

"Do the Germans see themselves as others see them?"

The result was a collection of interesting, thought provoking, and often amusing responses reflecting how the Germans see themselves and their fellow citizens.

Germans were asked to what extent they believe stereotypes such as punctuality, perfection and a lack of humour are true. They rated each one on a six point scale from strongly agree to strongly disagree. The respondents could also suggest a stereotype that in their opinion was missing from list of 13 characteristics:

(1) punctual, (2) hard-working, (3) perfectionistic, (4) efficient, (5) fluent in English, (6) sensitive concerning matters related to WW II, (7) reserved, (8) bureaucratic, (9) arrogant, (10) lacking humour, (11) direct, undiplomatic, (12) reliable, (13) honest.

91% of the respondents count Germany as their home with the remainder split between Austria, Switzerland and a smattering of other countries. 52% are men and 48% women, making it alamost a statistical tie between the sexes.

35% of the respondents are between 40 and 50 years of age, with another 24% in the next younger age bracket, between 30 and 40. Thus nearly 70% of the survey participants are in the 30 to 50 year age bracket; essentially people in their prime working years.

Birkenstocks, Beer and Bratwurst

By analysing the qualitative responses to the survey, we were able to see how some 2,000 Germans see themselves and to compare this to the global stereotype. To begin with, Germans eat unhealthily. Sauerkraut, sausages, potatoes, apple strudel and Black Forest cherry cake with cream. The portions are huge and so are the calories. Germans consume beer by the barrel. German women have hairy legs and underarms and men prefer to wear white socks together with Birkenstocks. Germans are everywhere. They are enthusiastic travellers who enjoy experiencing and learning about other cultures. On the other hand, once they discover a country, they descend like a plague of locusts, reserving entire sections of beach and marking their territories with towels. On the bright side, Germans are brilliant engineers who develop and produce innovative (but expensive) products that are valued throughout the world. They are highly educated, well-trained, inquisitive and even musically-adept.

Time is of the essence

One of the most revealing German television advertisements in recent years shows train passengers standing on a long platform at a typical German train station. The following announcement is broadcast over the intercom: "Ladies and gentlemen may I have your attention please. The Intercity Express to Hamburg will be three minutes late. Thank you for your patience." The train platform suddenly erupts into chaos. Passengers throw their hands in the air, look at their watches and hurl their luggage to the ground in frustration. Groups of enraged customers surround the train personnel and angrily point their fingers demanding action. This ad says a lot about the German psyche, but it mainly points to a key German characteristic: punctuality. More than 95% of the survey respondents view this as a typical German trait. Punctuality is more than a cliché in Germany; it's a way of life. Germans expect and demand promptness. If the post is usually delivered around 11:00 am, the local post office starts receiving calls at 11:07 a.m. asking where the postman is. An American acquaintance whose German wife rides the train to work each day told us: "Even if they stop the trains because emergency personnel have to attend to an injured person, my wife will shake her head in frustration and amazement. I always tell her that five-minute train delays in the U.S. are cause for celebration."

The survey participants were also asked to think about the trait of reliability, which is closely related to punctuality. Most of the survey respondents identify with this characteristic. Our friend Dieter, the breakfast roll hunter mentioned on page 15, is a good example. Not only is he punctual (he gets up at 6:30 am sharp!), he does it every day, exactly the same way. While on a small scale, it shows a cycle of reliability that is a foundation of German life. The service personnel at the bakery know that Dieter will come at 6:53. Dieter relies on the fact that the bakery is open and has his favourite rolls. Dieter's family can depend on him getting home with the rolls no later than 07:01. Everything works. Or as the Germans love to say, "Alles in Ordnung."

Teutonic perfection and efficiency

When asked why he chose a new printing press made by a German company, an American newspaper executive replied, "Because Germans are perfectionists." The survey participants were in full agreement. Whether this is viewed as a positive or negative trait depends on the situation. Most Germans have a great appreciation for this characteristic, especially when it comes to the quality of their cars and other products that are "Made in Germany." Apply this characteristic to the bureaucrat behind the counter at the local government office and suddenly the perfectionist is the devil in a jacket and tie. Germans take efficiency for granted. This is borne out by the survey, which shows that 87 %

of the respondents believe the stereotype of the efficient German is spot on. For instance, sometimes the escalators in the train stations appear to be out of order. But lightly treading on the first step magically brings it back to life. This is no miracle, rather an energy-saving design that illustrates how the German mind works. Visitors to Germany are sometimes amazed that train stations have no turnstiles and that people buy tickets on an honour system. This is not because Germans naturally trust people. It's because spot checks and immediate fines are more efficient than endless ticket queues and legions of ticket collectors.

All work and no play

An overwhelming number of the survey participants concur with the impression that the Germans are a hard working nation. After all, how else can a country rise from the ashes of a devastating war to become the world's third largest economy within a few decades? Hard work, attention to detail, organization and planning, competent and skilled, efficient; all of these traits are perceived to be prevalent in both the work and private lives of the typical German.

Brutally honest

The survey asks about two closely related traits: honesty and forthrightness. In both cases the respondents feel that Germans are generally candid, straightforward and not very diplomatic. To use an old English idiom, Germans don't like to beat around the bush. This is partly due to their infatuation with efficiency. Germans can be easily frustrated with the English habit of repeatedly prefacing requests with "Could you perhaps…" or "Would you be so kind as to…" In Germany there is a tendency to come to the point faster than in British English. We should also remember that being diplomatic in a foreign language requires a very high level of linguistic competence. Even if Germans want to speak or write more elaborately, a limited vocabulary limits their range of diplomatic expression.

Germany's past

When the participants were asked about the stereotype of the German who is uncomfortable with the country's past, specifically World War II, the responses were equally spread across the 6 rankings for the most part (only 4% did not agree at all). It should be noted that most of the respondents were born after World War II. Our own experience has shown that this age group understands and is sensitive about Germany's history, but does not feel directly responsible for it. Although Germans are gradually becoming more comfortable with the topic and can even joke about it sometimes, visitors should never make light of it. And when it comes to business relationships, the survey respondents make it clear that this subject is strictly off limits.

The arrogant German

The survey participants are divided as to what extent the stereotype of the arrogant German is true. It's interesting to note that only 6% fully agree with this cliché. But altogether, roughly 60% rated it as a valid German stereotype to some extent.

Humourless in Berlin

The most statistically-interesting traits relate to the humourless and reserved German. These pervasive clichés are frequently exploited in the media and especially in Hollywood. Apart from the obnoxious American in Bermuda shorts and baseball cap, the dour, grim-faced German is one of the most recognised stereotypes in the world. However, the survey respondents reject the notion that Germans are never funny, outgoing or sociable. Only 7% fully agree that

Germans lack a sense of humour and a mere 3% are ready to admit that Germans are restrained and quiet.

Germans do indeed have a sense of humour, but it often takes a German to understand it. The style varies from region to region. Bavarians are more vocal and outgoing and like to use their unique dialect as a form of humour. Rhinelanders have long-standing joke rituals stemming from the Karneval. Northern Germans in cities like Hamburg and Berlin tend towards an intellectual, dry and sarcastic form.

Prussian bureaucracy

The survey participants leave no doubt regarding their feelings about German bureaucracy. More than 90% of the respondents admit that this is a valid stereotype. One can also glean from the additional comments that it is viewed as a negative trait. Germans tend to complain about how much bureaucracy they have to deal with. On the other hand, they accept it as the price they have to pay for living in an orderly and disciplined society.

Sprechen Sie Englisch?

After the Dutch and the Swedes, Germans are probably the best English-as-a-second-language speakers in Europe. Numerically, the Germans are number one. First-time visitors to Germany are often astounded at Germans' command of English. So why are 41% of the survey respondents in disagreement with the stereotype of the German who is fluent in English?

Maybe this is related to German perfectionism. Native English speakers have lower standards, particularly when it comes to learning foreign languages. While Brits and Americans appreciate even the slightest attempt at English, the average German yearns to speak like a BBC newsreader, and when this fails, he begins to question his own ability.

Business, Romance, and Nationality

We asked the participants three open questions related to business, romance and nationality. These provided additional insight into how Germans view themselves. The comments underscore many of the clichés that appear in the international press.

Business Advice

In response to the question "What should foreigners take into consideration when conducting business with Germans?" the answer boils down to three words: Be on time! Punctuality runs like a long thread through the survey. 96% of the respondents rated punctuality as a typical German characteristic. So it is no surprise that this is considered a key trait that every foreign businessperson should bear in mind when sitting across the table from a German. Slipping into a meeting a few minutes late with a sheepish grin on your face won't help close that deal.

As the survey highlights, small talk is discouraged. As a matter of fact, there is no good German translation for "small talk." Business is business, private is private, and never the twain shall meet. One respondent put it bluntly: "We (Germans) talk in order to exchange information, not to develop relationships." Once in a meeting, the survey participants think it's better to write everything down. Germans want everything safely recorded. It provides a form of inner security. Said one respondent: "Document the meeting with minutes and be careful if the atmosphere starts becoming friendly."

German business people are the first to admit that hierarchy is ingrained in their business culture. The survey respondents point out that titles are important and that the boss should be treated like a boss. In America, a programmer at Microsoft would not hesitate to shake hands with a senior board member in the corridor and say, "Hi Bill, I'm John Smith." In Germany, such behaviour would be taboo. Finally, many of the participants emphasise the importance of maintaining a serious (professional) demeanour during business meetings ("Serious business people don't negotiate as if they were in a bazaar"). Still, they believe there is a time and place for everything. As one said, "Drinking a beer after closing a deal never hurt anyone." What better place is there than Germany to test this theory?

Pragmatic love

When it comes to love and marriage, the survey suggests that Germans shape up well as potential partners, albeit with a few caveats. Respondents were asked, "Have you ever had a partner who is of another nationality? Of your German traits, which did your partner particularly like or dislike?"

This answer reveals the paradox of being German:

"My partner appreciates that I'm reliable, orderly, and straightforward. But these same traits can be to my disadvantage in other situations."

Many respondents said their foreign-national partners criticised them for their fastidiousness, fanatic attention to detail and orderliness, yet admired traits such as hard-working, good planning and organisation skills. The survey indicates that some foreign nationals learn to take the good with the bad. An American business acquaintance once told us that his German wife drives him crazy with her obsessive sorting of the laundry; blue 30 degrees, 60 degrees white, 40 degrees mixed and so on. But he admitted that his clothes are always sparkling clean and that he has never had a white shirt suddenly turn Barbie pink.

Although the survey statistics indicate that Germans are sometimes lacking in the romance department (traits such as romantic, tender, sexy and passionate were infrequently mentioned), pragmatism eventually wins out. One respondent said his Croatian in-laws "rhapsodise about the fact that I'm not macho, that I work hard around the house and that I don't let my wife wait on me hand and foot." German women get high marks from their foreign national partners for their culinary skills and emancipated lifestyle. But one female respondent said her Italian husband didn't like the fact that German women tend to speak their minds.

Vive la France!

American poet Ralph Waldo Emerson once wrote, "The German intellect wants the French sprightliness, the fine practical understanding of the English, and the American adventure." In other words, they yearn most for what they don't have. To find out what Germans might be missing, we asked, "Which nationality would you prefer to have, had you not been born German, and why?"

At the top of the wish list is France. This response would have been unthinkable 50 to 100 years ago. But times change, new generations are born and attitudes shift. The post World War II generation does not carry the same burden as its parents.

But why does France appeal to today's German? The survey respondents cited the French way of life and the beautiful language. Here we can read between the lines. Despite having a strong work ethic, perhaps Germans don't fully buy the "all work, no play" concept. Maybe they secretly long for two-hour business lunches complete with wine. Instead of the daily trip to the recycling centre to ensure Ordnung, maybe Germans really dream about an early-evening stroll down the Champs-Élysées or sitting on a blanket on the banks of the Seine listening to Edith Piaf on an iPod.

The allure of the French language might be puzzling to some. But they say French is the language of love. With all due respect to Goethe and Schiller, we don't make the same association with the German language. German is technical, it's efficient. It boasts single (and long) words to describe complex philosophies, but no-one would call it the language of love. An Audi TV ad once poked fun at romantic dialogue in German cinema, a couple on a bridge are engaged riveting conversation "Hans! Helga! Hans!" while in the background an Audi 500 perfectly negotiates a slippery street.

Rule Britannia!

After French, the Germans would love to be British. Many Germans admire the British for their easy-going nature and well-known, often biting and black sense of humour (If you live in a country where it rains 150 to 200 days a year, humour is sometimes the only relief). The wacky humour of personalities such as John Cleese (Monty Python) and Rowan Atkinson (Mr. Bean), or fictional characters like Sherlock Holmes or James Bond have established British culture firmly in the German psyche.

La Dolce Vita!

Apart from France and the UK, Germans also like the idea of being Italian because of "La dolce vita," the life of luxury. And of course the food. It also helps that Italy is in southern Europe where many Germans would prefer to be in mid-November. The survey participants are also fond of the U.S.A. The reasons are many-fold, but like the British, the relaxed lifestyle is appealing. In addition, compared to Germany, Americans have less bureaucracy to deal with.

Over the years, Germans have entertained us with stories of holidays, business trips and extended stays in other countries. They rave about the wide-open spaces in America, the gorgeous hills of Tuscany and the chic streets of Monaco. But they gladly come home.

To put it another way, the grass is greener on the other side. The problem for the average German is, it's not always mowed.

Statistics

Generally speaking GERMANS are:	Pro		
	1	**2**	**3**
Punctual	32%	51%	13%
Hard-working	20%	43%	28%
Perfectionistic	24%	46%	22%
Efficient	18%	41%	28%
Fluent in English	3%	17%	39%
Sensitive concerning matters related to World War II	15%	25%	25%
Reserved	3%	15%	32%
Bureaucratic	39%	38%	15%
Arrogant	6%	21%	31%
Lacking Humour	7%	19%	27%
Direct, Undiplomatic	14%	33%	27%
Reliable	23%	52%	19%

1 = completely agree ... 6 = completely disagree

Contra

Total Result

4	5	6	Pro	Contra
2%	2%	0%	96%	4%
6%	2%	1%	91%	9%
5%	2%	1%	92%	8%
9%	3%	1%	87%	13%
27%	11%	3%	59%	41%
17%	14%	4%	65%	35%
26%	18%	6%	50%	50%
5%	2%	1%	92%	8%
22%	15%	5%	58%	42%
20%	21%	6%	53%	47%
15%	8%	3%	74%	26%
4%	1%	1%	94%	6%

Appendix

The Authors

Paul Smith

Back in the 1970s Paul was one of some 35,000 Smiths living in the greater London area, a good enough reason to migrate to Germany. Since then, he has consulted many large German companies.

His German still sounds rather English and his English is becoming German, one day these two languages will meet. He enjoys Schweine-krustenbraten with Colman's mustard.

Paul now lives in the country, between Munich and Zurich, where he is happy to be the only Smith within a 50 mile radius.

Ken Taylor

Ken has trained and eaten his way around the world – the raw heart of a cobra in Vietnam; caterpillars and maggots in Zambia; rotten, fermenting herring in Sweden. His favourite German dish is Sauermagen.

Now he lives in London where he enjoys eating eel, pie and mash. He continues teaching communication skills and writing books and articles.

His lucky number is 3.

Acknowledgements

We are indebted to many people who over the years, have contributed stories and insights which have shaped our perception of Germany. In particular, Ernst Baumann, Winfried Berner, Ron Beyma, Dagmar Beyrich, Dr Friedrich Blase, Jörg Bohn, Peter Born, Antony Burnet Smith, Riet Cadonau, Dr Ivar Cooke, Craig Collins, John Doorbar, Peter Duerig, Ralph Ehmann, Albrecht Enders, Jürgen Goebel, Alexander Gross, Dr Andreas and Renate Grossmann, Charis Hautzinger, Dr Harald and Marion Heck, Dr Christian Hort, Richard Howell, Walter Huempfner, Prof. Richard Joyce, Colin Kennard, Andreas König, H.G. Kraft, Dr Toby and Heidi Leber, Dr Luis and Margit Loracher, Uli Loth, Jürgen Ludwig, Andreas Luebbers, Dr Bruce Minor, Clyde Moss, Elfriede Orda, Dr Harald Oster, Dr Helmut Panke, Dr Christian Rauda, Dr Detlef Reeker, Wolfgang Robinow, Dr Lutz Schemperg, Elisabeth Scherer, Bernhard Seemüller, Herby Thurn, Nick Walker, Heiner Wendling, Robin Widdowson, Max Worcester, and many more who we did not mention.

Special thanks to our friends Cornelia Engelhard, Bernard (Bernie) Foerth, Dan and Sabine Hawpe, Ian McMaster, Thomas Rieger, Stefan Schiessl and Dieter Walther, for their help in reading the first draft and giving us their suggestions, corrections and comments.

Cornelia also aggregated and collated the survey results in German. Bernie designed the cover and drew the cartoons. Dan proof-read the original text and drafted the English version of the survey results. Stefan was responsible for the layout and design. Thanks again.

We are very grateful to Dr Moritz Hagenmüller and Annika Ollmann at Books On Demand for production within a ridiculously short timeframe.

Thanks also to our wives and partners Helga and Christine, for their support and work in the background. Any mistakes in the final draft are probably where we ignored their advice.

Paul Smith & Ken Taylor

CPSIA information can be obtained at www.ICGtesting.com
Printed in the USA
BVOW012100110412

287466BV00006B/257/P